MARTHA BUNNY LOVES SCHOOL

Clara Vulliamy

ALBERT WHITMAN & COMPANY
CHICAGO, ILLINOIS

For the real
Martha
with love

Library of Congress Cataloging-in-Publication
data is on file with the publisher.
Text and illustrations copyright
© 2012 by Clara Vulliamy
Published in 2013 by Albert Whitman & Company
ISBN 978-0-8075-4976-6
First published in 2012 in Great Britain
by HarperCollins Children's Books.
Printed in China.
10 9 8 7 6 5 4 3 2 1 SC 18 17 16 15 14 13

For more information about
Albert Whitman & Company,
visit our web site at
www.albertwhitman.com.

This is a

happy book all about

MARTHA—

that's me!

A few very important things about me, just so you know...

my **favorite** color is **yellow**

and my **favorite** popsicle is **pink**...

I like d👁️👁️dling

and scootering

decorating my own cookies

and

and trampolining...

and my

starry
sunglasses
(because I like to see the world all rosy!)

I **love** my snow globe

but my yellow-and-blue-
and-orange-and-pink
polka-dot rain boots are what

I love best!

I **never** take
them off, not even in bed!

News!
Today is my first
day at school!

I am very excited about starting school, but there is one **huge** problem…

my bunny brothers!

Here's Monty.
His favorite color is red
and he's crazy about robots
and rockets
and dinosaurs.
He's always full of energy and
he talks **all the time**!

And here's Pip.
He's the baby.
He doesn't say muc

They will both really miss me!

Oh, and this is our puppy, Paws.

Of all the pets

on our street, pets

Paws is **by far** the naughtiest.

But I'd better get ready—Mom is calling us for breakfast. She says, "Get a move on, Martha!"

"Sit down, Monty! Sit down, Pip!" I say. Mom says
I need a nice, big breakfast for my first day at school!

I have cereal — a banana — and orange juice

Monty has toast — with jam — and apple juice

and Pip has French toast sticks — an egg — and milk

Monty will only eat his breakfast inside his box and Pip
is squeezing egg through his fingers. "Mud!" says Pip.

What *funny bunnies* they are!

And now I'm getting dressed. I want to wear something **very special** for school but I don't know what to choose...

they

are

all my

favorites!

Now I'm ready!

But wait—best of all, I have a **fantastic** new school bag! Inside it has one big pocket and lots of little pockets to put all my things in.

"What's that, Martha?" asks Monty.

I say, "It's my new school bag."

Monty says,
"Can we go to school too?
Me and Pip and Paws?
We can go in your bag—
we can squeeze!"

"But you are still little. One day you will be big enough,"
I say, "but today only **I** am just the right size for school."

Once I was
very little

then I was
little

and now I am
BIG

Sometimes I think about what I'd like to do when I'm huge...

make hats

and drive a bus

and be a diver

and have
a bakery

and be a vet

And sorry, Paws.
DEFINITELY
no puppies
in school!

My bunny brothers are looking really sad.

"But what will we do, Martha, while you're at school?" asks Monty.

Luckily I have a brilliant idea. Let's set up the

Happy Bunny Club!

"Hooray!" shouts Monty.
"Hooray!" shouts Pip.
"Hooray, hooray!" shouts Monty.

"…What is a club?"

"It's a very exciting thing that you are **in**," I say.
"Like a box?" says Monty.
"A **little** like a box, but not completely," I say,
"and it happens in a **SECRET DEN!**"

The **DEN** needs:

**comfy
cushions**

**Monty's
toys**

**Pip's
zebra**

games

music

**apples for
a snack**

Sorry, Paws,
no puppies in the
club. You'd make
a mess!

"Squash!" says Pip.

"It's not
a squash,"
says Monty
"It's cozy!"

"Do you like it?
Are you happy?"
I ask.
"GREAT!"

Now I need to get ready for school because Mom is calling, **"Ten minutes** to go, Martha!"

But Monty says, "Don't go—we need a sign for the den!"

So I make a sign in my best grown-up writing.

It says,

Happy Bunny Club
that is fun and games
for two left-behind bunnies

This bit was chewed by Paws

Now I start packing my bag for school.
I choose a few of my favorite things to take...

one or two books

my recorder

my old bear

I've had this bear since I w JUST BOR.

some

of

my

smaller

knickknack

and **of course** my snow globe

and
my

starry
sunglasses.

Now
my bag
is a **little full.**

But the little  bunnies still  follow me

everywhere.

 "Are those my fairy wings, Monty?" I say.

"No, these aren't your fairy wings, Martha," says Monty.

These are my *super-speedy-flyers* for going all around the world!

I **need** them for the club!"

I need my **best supplies** from my craft box to fill my bag, but I don't know what to choose...

they are **all** my best!

Paws, come back here with that ribbon!

Now my bag is **very full**...

Here are the little bunnies— **AGAIN.**

Monty says, "We need a special badge to show we are in the Happy Bunny Club."

"Too busy!" I say.

"Please!" says Monty.

"Peas!" says Pip.

So I make a badge for Monty...

"Now I really need to get ready, little bunnies!" I say.

and a badge for Pip.

I **need**

a pencil,

and a ruler

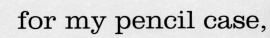

an eraser,

for my pencil case,

but when I look
for my best pens…

they've completely
disappeared!

you

have

"Do

my

in

best

pens

there?"

I ask

Happy Bunny Club
that is fun and games
for two left-behind bunnies

that is fun and games
for two left-behind bunnies

"No, we don't have them, Martha," says Monty.

"I really **need** them for school," I say,

but there's no time because Mom is saying,

"Five minutes, Martha!"

Quick! **I need to hurry!**

I need...

my coat!

My scarf!

My gloves!

Just a few more things!

My arm floats!

My crown!

My flashlight!

Now my
bag is
too full
to zip up.

Luckily
I have
lots of
pockets!

My scooter!

My hula-hoop!

My hat!

My flag!

Now I'm ready to go...

But— Squeeze!

I can't fit through the front door.

Mom says,
"Gosh, Martha—you can't take all that stuff to school!"

I don't know what to do.

Today is my first day at school
and I can't even take all my favorite things.
And where are my bunny brothers?

"Martha, Martha, we made this for you—it's your Happy Bunny Club badge!"

I love it!

Mom says,

"One more minute, Martha!"

So I unpack my bag and I put in my Happy Bunny Club badge. It's all I really need.

"You can look after my snow globe, Pip," I say,

"and you can look after my starry sunglasses, Monty."

"I know you will **really** miss me, little bunnies," I say, "but be brave!"

Happy Bunny Club
that is fun and games
for two left-behind bunnies

"And look after the den until I get home!"

While I'm at school having **fun**, I know my bunny brothers are.

waiting…

waiting…

waiting…

until—

"I'm back!"

They go **crazy** with joy to see me!

"I love school,"

I them, "and I got lots of great stuff...

kind helper

great work!

1 2 3

But look—I still have my Happy Bunny Club badge!

Let's go into the den!"

I squash up with my
bunny brothers because…

…I know they can't really have a

Happy Bunny Club

without…

me!

"But what should we do about Paws?" asks Monty. "He's **desperate** to join in!"

Luckily Happy Bunnies never leave anyone out, so I say...

"OK, Paws, you can join the club!"

The End!